THE BACKYARD
BUILD

(Engineering)

Written by
Jonathan Litton

Illustrated by
Magalí Mansilla

Suzy and Max sat in the yard looking glum. The swing was broken, the soccer ball was flat, and their kite was stuck up a tree!

"We don't have anything
to play with," said Suzy.
"What shall we do?"
"I don't know," replied
Max, gloomily.

Just then, they heard a noise
from Miss Gizmo's yard next door.
They peeped over the fence.

"Miss Gizmo has built a bird
bath—how cool!" said Max. "Maybe
she could help us fix the old swing?"
"Great idea, Max," said Suzy. "Let's ask her."

"It's amazing what you can do with an old broom handle and a tray," said Miss Gizmo to herself.

SPLISH! SPLASH!

5

Suzy and Max asked
Miss Gizmo to help.

"Of course!" she replied.
"I'll bring my tools over,
but you will have to design
and build the swing yourselves!"

"Great! I can just picture how the new swing will look," said Max.

"We've got some wood and things we could use! What shall we do first?" asked Suzy.

Suzy found a plank of wood for the swing. "This is the right size and shape to make a good, strong seat," she said.

"What shall we use to hang the swing from the tree?" asked Miss Gizmo. "Shall we use the old rope or this chain?"

"This rope doesn't feel very strong," said Max, pulling on it. "Let's try the chain."

"You're right, Max," said Miss Gizmo. "If I pull hard on the rope it might break, but the chain won't."

WHEEEEEE!

Miss Gizmo made two holes in the wood, then she fixed the chain to the seat with screws. Max and Suzy took turns trying out the swing. It worked!

"What would you like to build next?" asked Miss Gizmo.

"Let's make a seesaw!" suggested Suzy. "We could use this old plank and tree trunk! How do we make it balance?"

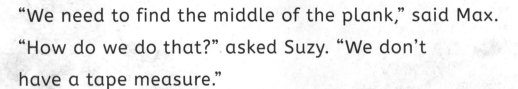

"We need to find the middle of the plank," said Max.
"How do we do that?" asked Suzy. "We don't
have a tape measure."

"Maybe we could use our hands to
measure how long it is?" said Max.
"If the plank is 30 hands long, then
we know that 15 hands is halfway."

"That's right!" said Miss Gizmo.

YEE-HAW!

They balanced the plank of wood on top of the tree trunk. Miss Gizmo added two small logs to keep the plank in place.

13

Next, Suzy and Max gathered materials to make a slide.

"Shall we use bricks for the steps?" asked Suzy.
"Good idea," said Miss Gizmo.
"What will you use for the slide?"

Max pointed to a sheet of plywood leaning up against the shed.
"What about that?" he asked.

"Maybe," said Miss Gizmo. "But do you think the wood will be slippery enough?"

"This sheet of plastic looks super-slippery!" said Suzy.

15

"Plastic is much smoother," said Miss Gizmo.
"And you won't get any splinters!" she laughed.

But although the plastic was
slippery, Max couldn't slide down.
"Why can't I slide, Miss Gizmo?" asked Max.

Miss Gizmo chuckled. "It looks like we have another design problem to fix. What do you think we should do?" she asked.

"Let's make it steeper!" said Suzy and she added a few more bricks to the steps.

Together, they moved the top of the slide to a higher position. The slide worked perfectly!

Just as they finished building their
playground, rain clouds appeared in the sky.

19

"Oh dear," said Miss Gizmo. "I haven't finished my bird bath—it needs a roof!" And she hopped over the wall.

Suzy and Max swung and seesawed and slid until the rain started. "Let's build a roof for our playground tomorrow," they said.

WHAT CLEVER LITTLE ENGINEERS THEY ARE!

The engineering behind the story

Let's look at some of the problems Suzy and Max had to solve in the story. Turn to the page numbers for help, or find the answers on the next page.

p.7

Making a plan

When you want to build something, it's important to have a plan.

Before they fixed the swing, what did Suzy and Max have to decide first?

Your turn

Some playgrounds have climbing walls. What materials would you need to build it? What tools would be useful? What design problems might you come across and how would you solve them?

p.8

Choosing materials

Materials have different properties that make them useful for different tasks.

What did Suzy use to make a seat for the swing?

p.9

Why did Max decide the chain was better than the rope?

Your turn

What else would make a good seat for a swing? How did Miss Gizmo and Max test the rope and the chain? What materials do you think are good for building a boat, or a house?

p.12

Problem solving

When you want to make something, think about the problems first, then find different solutions to fix them.

How did Suzy and Max measure the plank of wood?

Your turn

Can you think of other ways Suzy and Max could have measured the plank of wood?

Answers

If you need help finding the answers, try reading the page again.

Making a plan: Suzy and Max had to decide what the swing would look like, and what materials they would use to build it.

Choosing materials: Suzy found a plank of wood for the seat. Max decided to use the chain to hang the swing from the tree because it was stronger than the rope.

Problem solving: Suzy and Max used their hands to measure the length of the wooden plank, and find its center.

Quarto is the authority on a wide range of topics.

Quarto educates, entertains and enriches the lives of our readers—enthusiasts and lovers of hands-on living.

www.quartoknows.com

Author: Jonathan Litton
Illustrator: Magalí Mansilla
Consultant: Ed Walsh
Editors: Jacqueline McCann, Carly Madden, Ellie Brough
Designer: Sarah Chapman-Suire

© 2018 Quarto Publishing plc

First published in 2018 by QEB Publishing,
An imprint of The Quarto Group
6 Orchard Road, Suite 100
Lake Forest, CA 92630
T: +1 949 380 7510
F: +1 949 380 7575
www.QuartoKnows.com

A CIP record for this book is available from the Library of Congress.

ISBN 978 1 78603 281 2

9 8 7 6 5 4 3 2 1

Manufactured in Dongguan, China
TL052018

MIX
Paper from responsible sources
FSC www.fsc.org FSC® C104723

Find out more...

Here are links to websites where you will find more information on engineering, from planning to building.

PBS Kids
www.pbskids.org/cyberchase/find-it/science-and-engineering/

Ecosystems for Kids
www.ecosystemforkids.com/materials.html